For Jessica and Charlie

Copyright © 2022 by Briony May Smith

All rights reserved. Published in the United States by Anne Schwartz Books,
an imprint of Random House Children's Books, a division of Penguin Random House LLC, New York.

Anne Schwartz Books and the colophon are trademarks of Penguin Random House LLC.

Visit us on the Web! rhcbooks.com

Educators and librarians, for a variety of teaching tools, visit us at RHTeachersLibrarians.com

Library of Congress Cataloging-in-Publication Data is available upon request.
ISBN 978-1-9848-9656-8 (trade) — ISBN 978-1-9848-9657-5 (lib. bdg.) — ISBN 978-1-9848-9658-2 (ebook)

The text of this book is set in 14-point Garamond Premier Pro Medium.
The illustrations were rendered in mixed media.
Book design by Nicole de las Heras

MANUFACTURED IN CHINA
10 9 8 7 6 5 4 3 2 1
First Edition

The MERMAID MOON

Briony May Smith

a·s·b
anne schwartz books

Once, there were two best friends.
One was from the sea—a mermaid named Merrin.
And one was from the land—a human named Molly.

Molly lived in Merporth, a little fishing village, where the houses were stacked around the harbor and the boats went up and down with the tide. She could see the sea from her bedroom window.

Merrin lived in the harbor with her mom, Nerissa,
who protected the cove from the wind and rain. She
taught Merrin whale songs and storm charming to keep
her safe. When the sun set, they fell asleep inside their
mermaid cave carved into the harbor wall.

Every day after school, the girls would play together, Molly above the water and Merrin below.

They'd search for treasure in sea caves and ancient shipwrecks.

They'd surf the waves with the dolphins, and follow pods of whales as they glided through the gloomy depths.

One afternoon, the girls watched excitedly as Merporth bustled with preparations. That night was the Mermaid Moon festival, and Merrin was finally old enough to join in! All the sea creatures would be able to swim through the air to explore the human world. Best of all, Merrin would see Molly's house for the first time.

Molly skipped home for dinner. "Keep it real, baby seal!" she called. "See you tonight!"

"Farewell, seashell!" Merrin replied, diving below the water.

After eating their seaweed supper, Merrin's mom told her
more about the Mermaid Moon.

"Make sure to be home before the moon's reflection disappears from
the sea, my little minnow," she warned. "Otherwise, your scales will dry
out, and the magic will vanish from the cove forever."

Merrin gulped and nodded. Then Nerissa wrapped her fin around her daughter, saying, "But don't forget to have fun!"

As the moon started to rise, Merrin watched the first creatures lift out of the waves. Seals twisted and turned in the night sky. Dolphins leapt and stayed airborne, flicking their tails to propel them to town.

Merrin closed her eyes and concentrated on the Mermaid Moon
magic. She pushed up to the surface . . .

. . . and kept on going, up and up and up!
She swished her glittering fin and followed the flurry of fish,
swimming through the air with a bright laugh.

At the water's edge, Merrin spotted Molly waiting for her.

"You're flying!" Molly giggled. "Come on! There's so much to see, and Mom and Dad said you could sleep over!"

Merrin floated to a stop. "I wish I could, but . . ." And she explained what her mother had told her about the Mermaid Moon magic vanishing.

Molly's face fell, but then she smiled. "Oh well," she declared. "We better get going then!"

The streets of Merporth were strung with seashell bunting, coral wreaths hung on doors, and sea glass mobiles sparkled in windows. Fish scales shimmered and twinkled in the moonlight. There were market stalls and even a band, and Merrin swam among it all, enchanted.

At one stall, Molly bought them matching bracelets
with her allowance.

At another, Merrin tried her first hot chocolate.

As the moon began to sink and the market closed,
the girls wandered up the hill to Molly's house. They went
silently upstairs, careful not to wake her mom and dad.

To Merrin, Molly's room seemed full of strange things. Merrin stared at the coral-less walls and frowned in confusion at the lamp, until Molly flicked the light switch.

"Wow," whispered Merrin.

Instead of a sandy seabed, there was a fluffy carpet, and instead of sea kelp, blankets. There were books, toys, paper, and pens, along with things they had collected together— jars of sea glass and shells on every shelf.

When she saw the moon glint through the bedroom curtains,
Merrin said, "Uh-oh, I'd better head home."

Down the stairs and out of the door the girls hurried.
But in Molly's backyard, something caught Merrin's eye.

"What's that?" Merrin asked.

"My swing," Molly replied. "Want a try?"

"Yes, please!" cried Merrin, climbing on.

Molly pushed.

"It's like swimming and flying all at once!" Merrin exclaimed.

When the swing slowed to a stop, she looked up at the moon with a sigh. She really didn't want to leave yet.

An owl swooped overhead, and Merrin floated up to a tree branch to watch it fly beyond the hills.

Molly clambered up after her—and noticed the moon was starting to dip into the sea. "Quick!" she reminded Merrin. "You need to get home!"

"Oh, sea urchins!" Merrin said. "I wish I could stay forever." And she drifted sadly down.

But as Molly followed, shimmying down the tree, the branch
beneath her foot *snapped*. She clung to the branch above, stuck.
Merrin rushed over to help.

She clasped Molly's hand and pulled, but she could feel the magic wearing off. There was no way she could carry Molly down.

"Go, Merrin, or you'll be stuck too!" urged Molly.

"I won't leave without you!" said Merrin as her scales started to tingle. But if she stayed, she'd ruin the magic of the Mermaid Moon. Oh, what should she do?

And then she remembered. There was a song her mom had taught her long ago, a whale song to sing in times of trouble. Closing her eyes, she began:

Whale, whale, great or small
Deep below the white sea foam
Listen, listen, hear my call
Mighty whale, please help me home . . .

The lilting melody pulsed through the air and sea.

Suddenly, from the depths beyond the harbor leapt a huge whale, pushing out of the waves into the sky. Water poured off its back onto the rooftops as it swooped toward them.

The whale hovered over the tree, holding its fin steady for the girls to climb on.

Molly gasped. "Don't be afraid," said Merrin, helping her friend mount the whale's back.

Once astride, the girls clung to its barnacles. With a swoosh of its tail, the whale set off again. Molly and Merrin cheered the great creature on as it hurtled through the sky to the sea.

With the Mermaid Moon magic wearing off, the whale skirted over chimneys and brushed past treetops.

It sank lower, narrowly missing the harbor wall. Molly slid off
just before Merrin and the whale splashed into the sea.

Merrin burst out of the water and flipped into the air. "We did it!" she cried.

In the distance, the whale's tail saluted them before sinking below.

"Goodbye!" called Molly. "Thank you!"

The moon's reflection twinkled on the waves for one last moment—and was gone.

Molly hugged her friend goodbye. "I can't wait for next year, when we can do it all again!" she said.

Merrin laughed and hugged Molly back. Then she dipped below the waves, to her mermaid cave, and Molly skipped up the hill, to her cottage, to sleep.

fin.